Another Sommer-Time Story™

King
of the Pond

By Carl Sommer
Illustrated by Greg Budwine

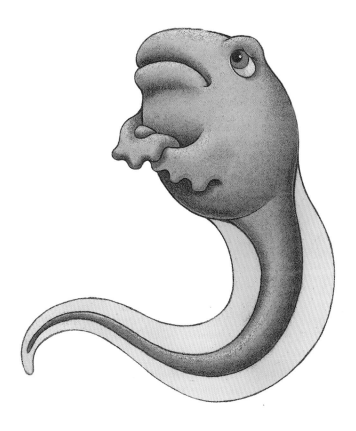

Advance
PUBLISHING, INC • HOUSTON

Copyright © 2000 by Advance Publishing, Inc.

Permissions
Advance Publishing, Inc.
6950 Fulton St.
Houston, TX 77022

www.advancepublishing.com

First Edition
Printed in Singapore

Library of Congress Cataloging-in-Publication Data

Sommer,1930-
   King of the Pond / by Carl Sommer; illustrated by Greg Budwine.--1st ed.
     p. cm. -- (Another Sommer-Time Story)
   Summary: Tombo, the biggest, fastest, and strongest tadpole in the pond, teases and
chases all the other tadpoles, but he comes to regret his bullying when he turns into the
smallest, slowest, and weakest frog.
   Cover title: Carl Sommer's The King of the Pond.
   ISBN 1-57537-016-6 (hardcover: alk. paper). -- ISBN 1-57537-065-4 (library binding:
alk. paper)
   [1. Tadpoles Fiction. 2. Frogs Fiction. 3. Bullies Fiction.] I. Budwine, Greg, ill. II
Title. III. Title: Carl Sommer's The King of the Pond. IV. Series: Sommer, Carl, 1930-
Another Sommer-Time Story.
PZ7.S696235Ki 2000   99-35284
[E]--dc21   CIP

Another Sommer-Time Story™

King
of the Pond

Tombo, the largest tadpole in the pond, made himself King of the Pond.

One day he barged into a group of playing tadpoles and boasted, "*I'm* the biggest, the fastest, and the strongest tadpole. *I'm* King of the Pond! Try to beat *me* in a race!"

Tilly swam up beside the noisy tadpole and said, "Tombo, when are you going to learn to stop breaking up our games? We were having lots of fun before you zoomed in."

Tombo got mad. He always wanted everyone
to play his games. Tombo was bigger and
stronger than the other tadpoles. And because

of his size, he would often tease the others by chasing them all around the pond. Then he would laugh at them as they swam away.

Often the tadpoles had races around the pond. And whenever they did, Tombo would always say, "Try to beat *me* in a race. *I'm* the biggest, the fastest, and the strongest tadpole. *I'm* King of the Pond!"

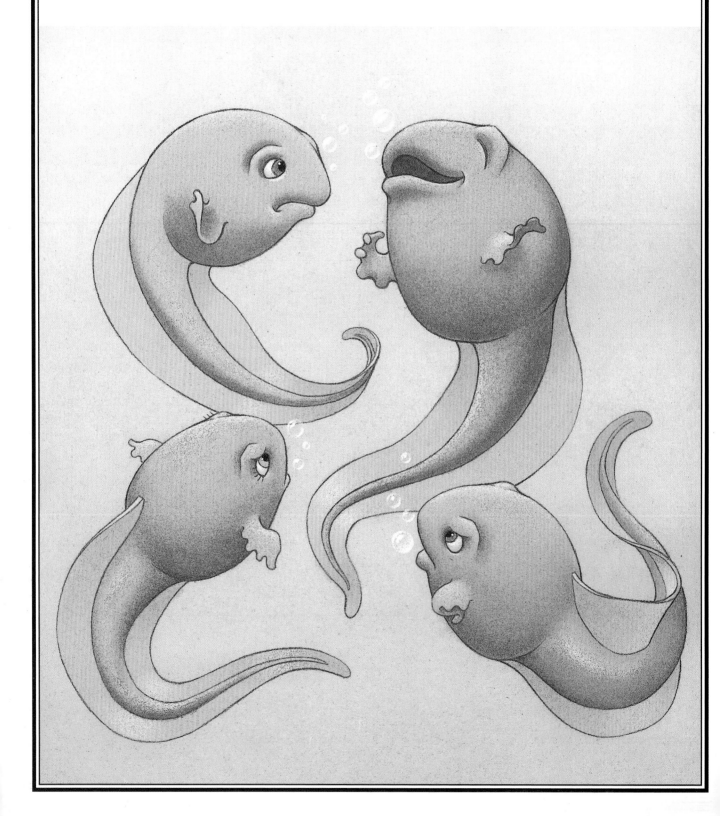

Tombo was right—he always won the races. And after every race, Tombo would boast, "Seeeeeee! Didn't I tell you *I'm* the biggest, the fastest, and the strongest tadpole in the pond? *I'm* King of the Pond!"

Whenever the tadpoles found food, Tombo would chase everyone away. He always demanded, "*I'm* the biggest, so *I'm* eating first!"

Tombo never shared his food with others. Only when *he* had enough to eat, then he would let the others eat.

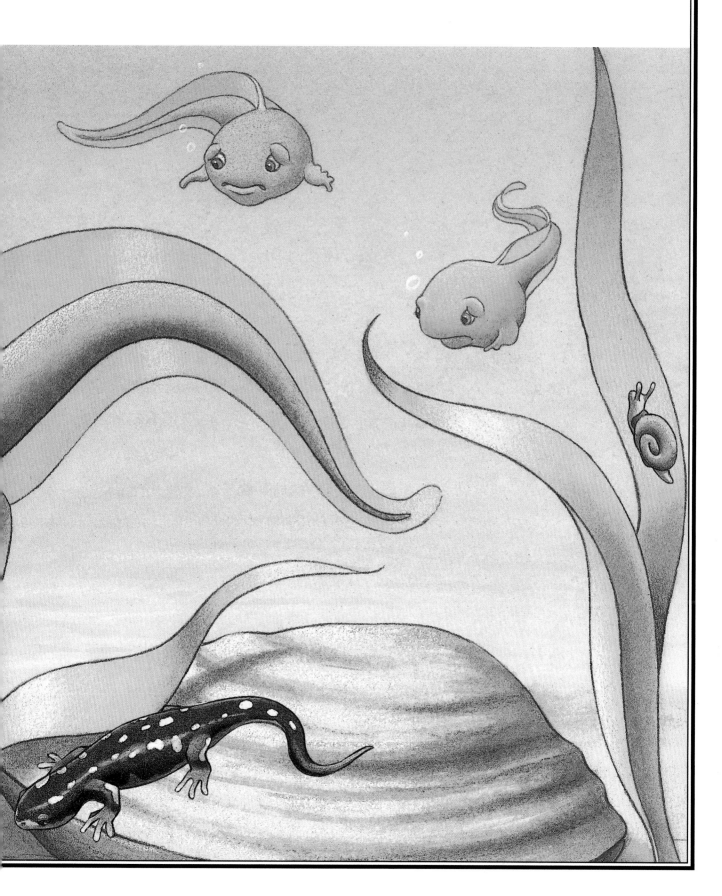

One day while they were racing, a big fish
suddenly appeared. All the tadpoles swam away
as fast as they could to hide.

But not Tombo—he knew he was fast. He
swam right in front of the big fish, stuck out his
tongue and sneered, "You can't catch *me*!"

The fish was furious. He made a quick dash to catch Tombo, but Tombo dove under a log.

Tombo peeked out from under the log, stuck out his tongue, and said, "I dare you to catch me!"

The fish made another dash to catch him, but

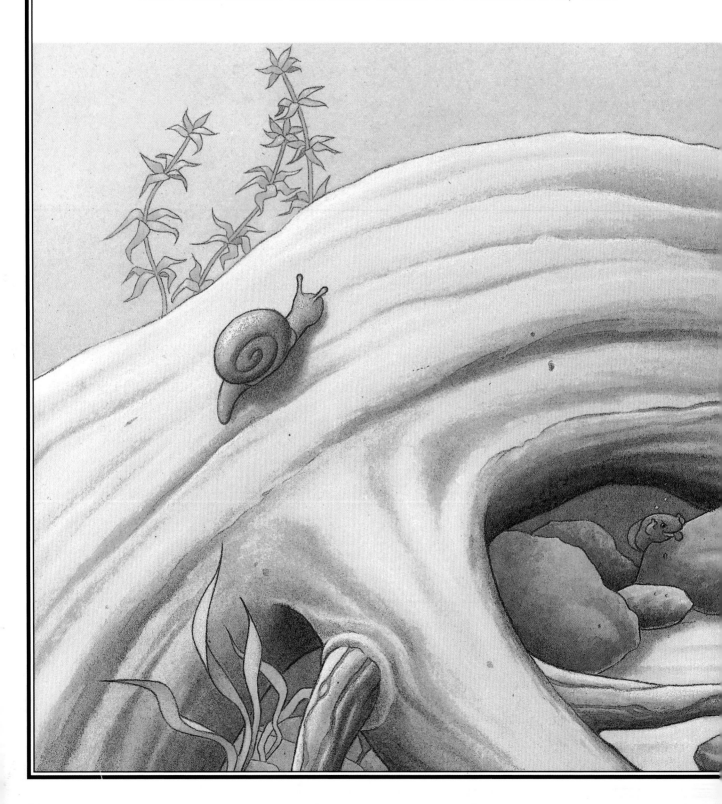

Tombo pulled in his head. He did this over and over again until the angry fish finally left.

Then Tombo swam to his friends and boasted, "*I'm* not afraid of anything! *I'm* the biggest, the fastest, and the strongest tadpole. *I'm* King of the Pond!"

Not only was Tombo the biggest, the fastest, and the strongest tadpole, but he could also do fancy tricks. One day Tombo said to his friends, "Watch *me*!"

Tombo swam fast and did a flip in the air.

"Wow!" said all the tadpoles. Everyone was impressed, except for Tilly.

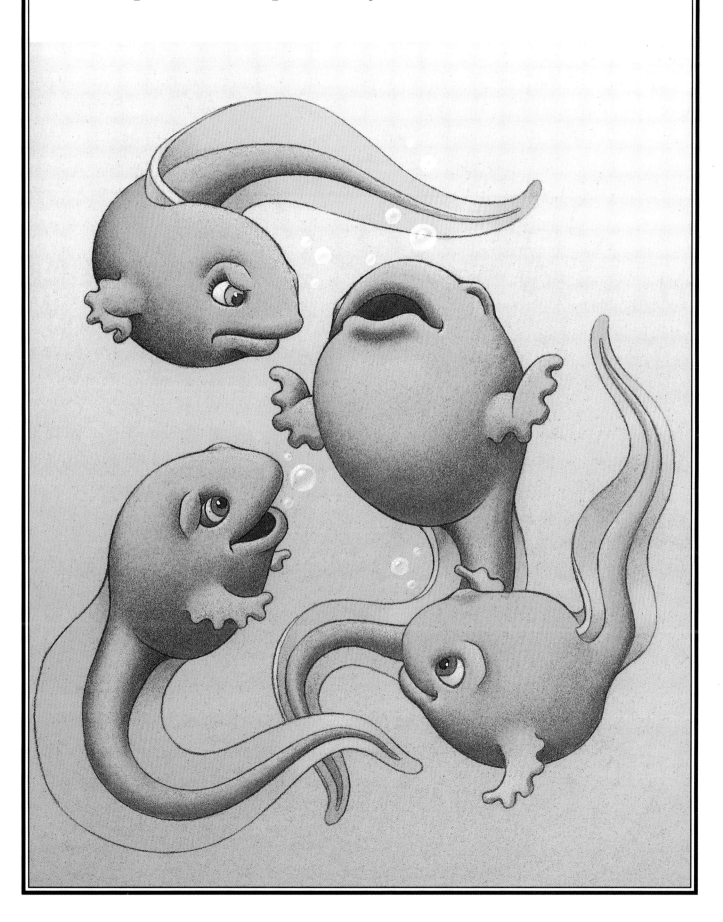

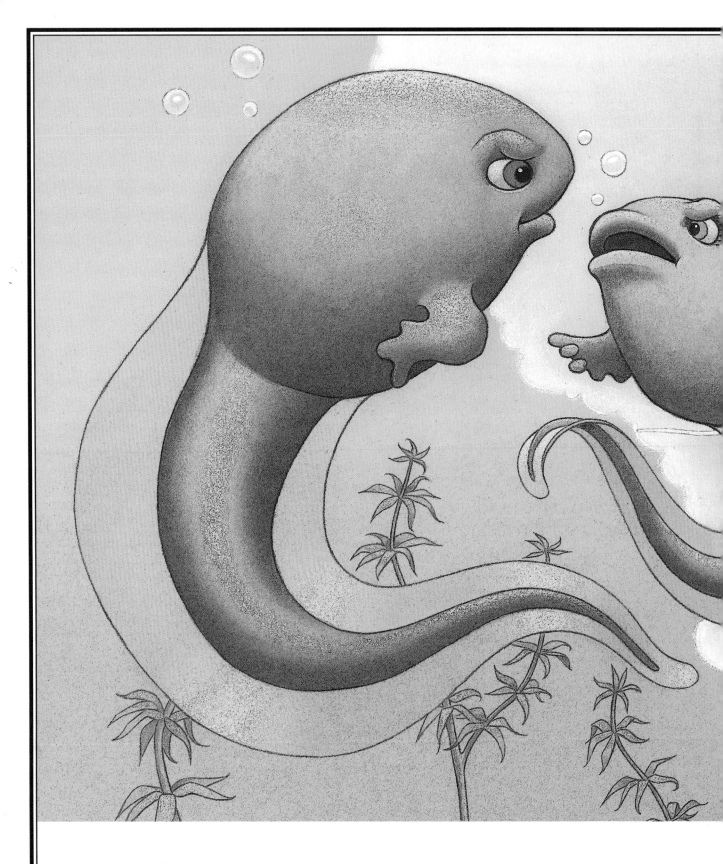

Tilly swam over to Tombo and said, "You better be careful. When you jump out of the water, a fish might have you for dinner or a bird might swoop down and swallow you up."

Tombo laughed and said, "They'll never catch *me*! *I'm* the biggest, the fastest, and the strongest tadpole. *I'm* King of the Pond! *I'm* not afraid of anything!"

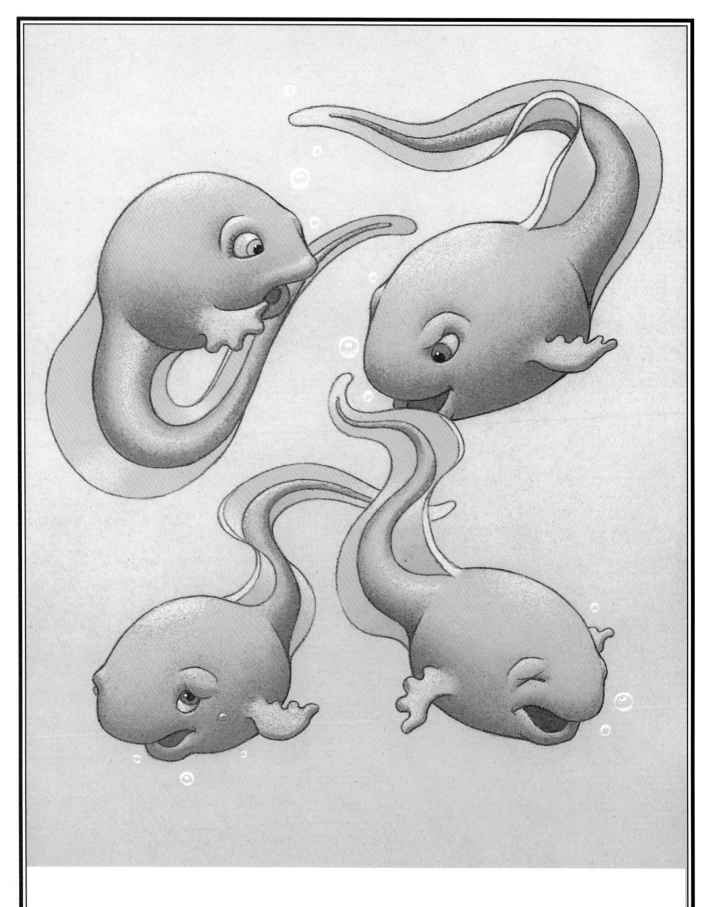

As Tombo became older, not only did he chase
the tadpoles, now he also nipped their tails.

When they yelled, "Ouch!" Tombo would laugh and laugh. He thought it was lots of fun when all the tadpoles dashed away from him when he pinched them.

Tombo became a big bully. As long as *he* had fun, he did not care about anyone else.

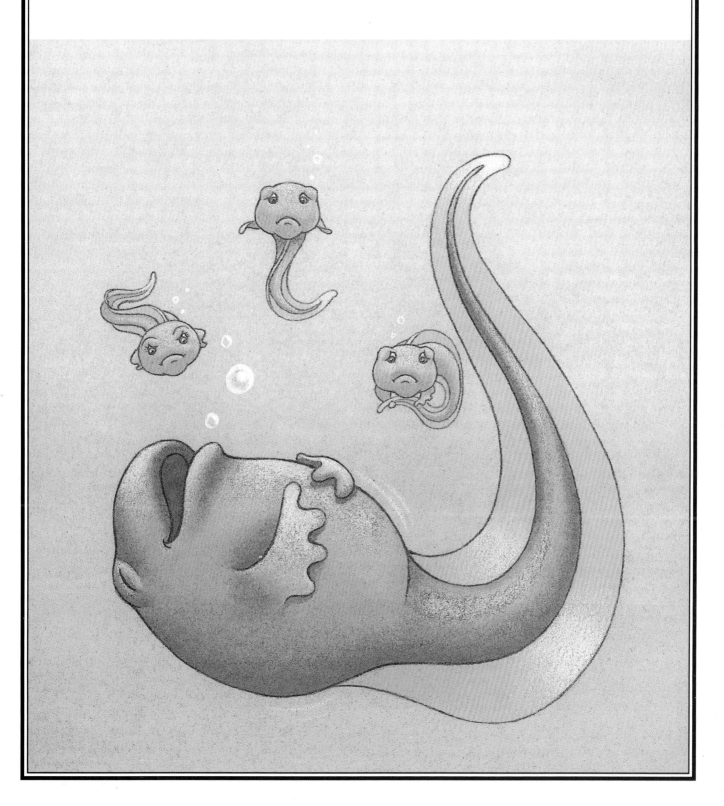

Freddy complained to Tilly, "It's just not fair for Tombo to treat us so badly. He's a big bully!"

Just then Tombo came along. Freddy and Tilly dashed under a log. As they were hiding under the log, Tilly said to Freddy, "Don't worry about Tombo. What goes around, comes

around. Bullies and boasters will get what they deserve."

"I certainly hope you're right," said Freddy. "But I don't see how. Tombo is the biggest, the fastest, and the strongest tadpole in the pond."

"Just wait and see," said Tilly.

One day Tombo said to the other tadpoles, "Look at my new trick. *I* can do a double flip."

Tombo swam fast. He flipped in the air, and then flipped again.

When he came back to the tadpoles, he stuck out his chest and said, "I bet none of you can even do one flip!"

All the tadpoles tried, but no one was able to do a single flip.

Meanwhile, at the other end of the pond, a boy named Alex was trying to catch some fish with his net. But when Alex saw Tombo jump out of the water, he said, "What was that?"

He tiptoed over to where Tombo had jumped. Then he laid down on the dock and held out his net.

Meanwhile under the water, Tombo laughed at his friends as they tried to do a flip. Then he bragged, "Seeeeeee! Didn't I tell you that *I'm* the only one who can do flips? *I'm* the biggest, the fastest, and the strongest tadpole! *I'm* King of the Pond! Do you want to see me do a triple flip?"

No one said a word.

"Watch *me*!"

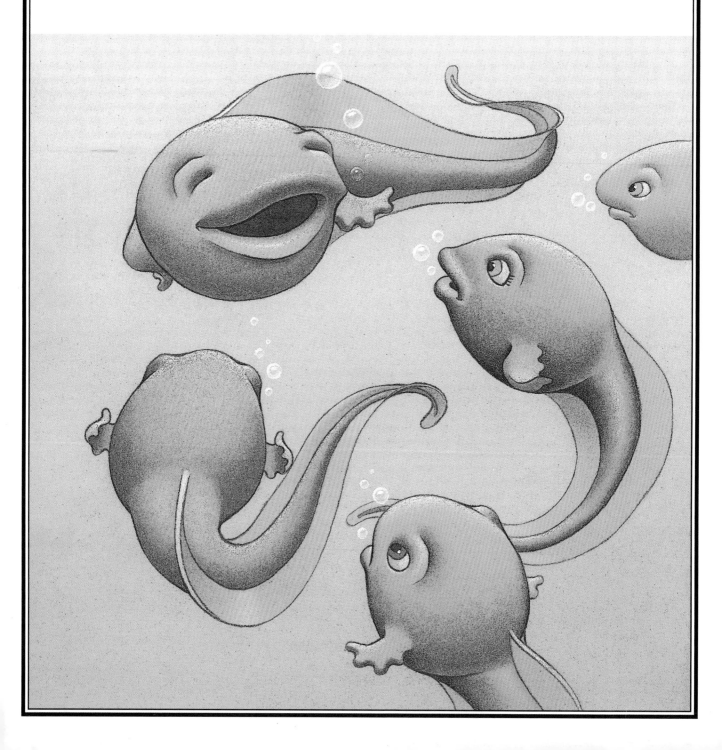

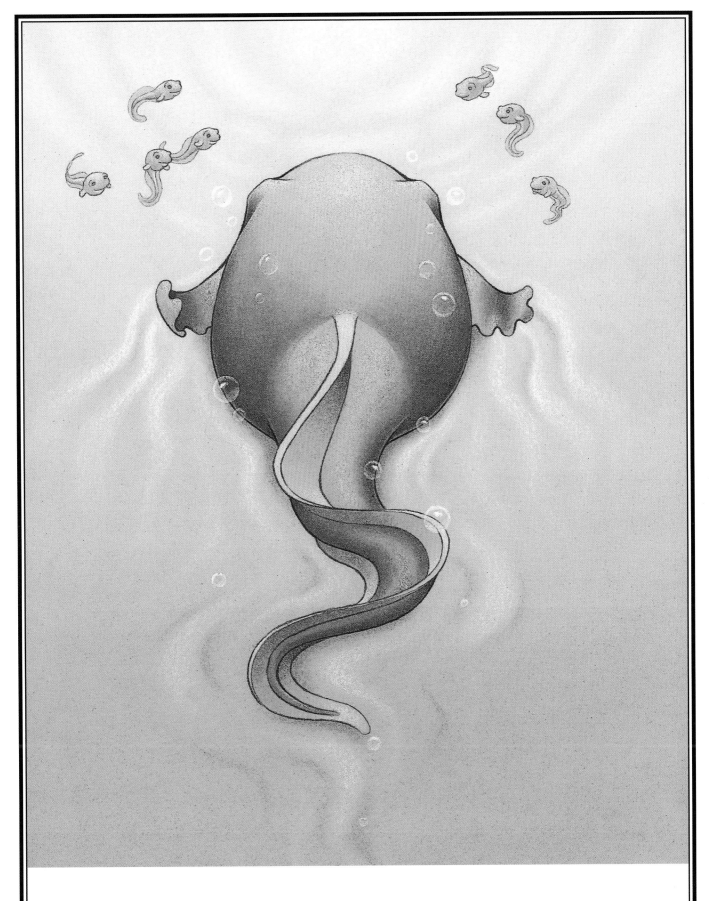

Tombo zoomed to the other end of the pond.
Then he swam back as fast as he could.

When Tombo leaped out of the water to do his triple flip, Alex had his net ready. Tombo flipped right into the net!

"Oh good!" yelled Alex as he quickly closed his hand around the net. Then he carefully put Tombo into his glass jar.

When Tombo did not land in the water, Freddy asked, "What happened to Tombo?"

"Probably a bird got him," said Tilly.

Alex ran back to his picnic table and yelled, "Dad, Mom, look what I caught!"

"That's just a little tadpole," said Dad.

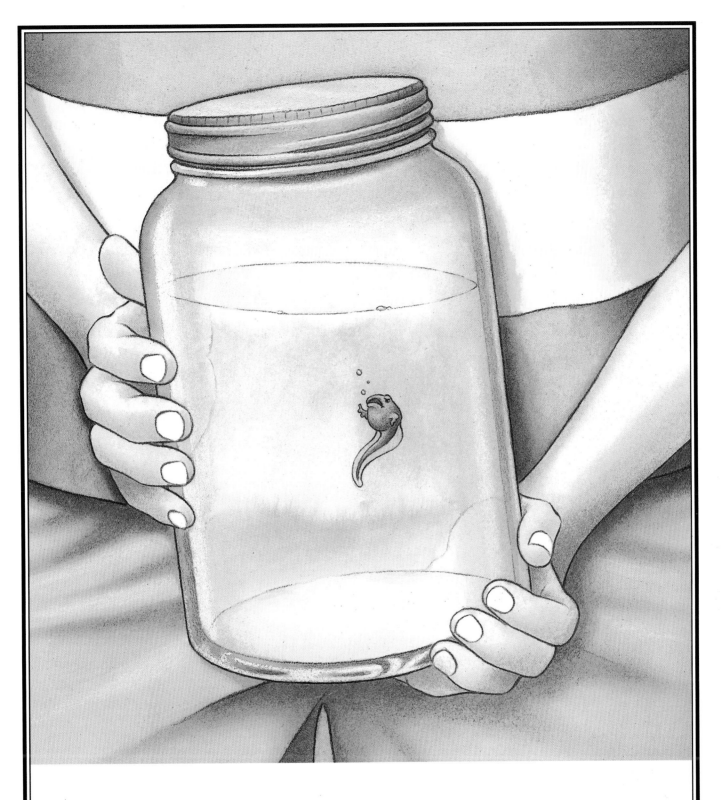

When Tombo heard that he was called "a little tadpole," he became furious.

"I'm not little," he yelled. "*I'm* the biggest, the fastest, and the strongest tadpole! *I'm* King of the Pond!"

But nobody heard him.

As they drove home from the picnic, Alex held
Tombo in his lap. Dad stopped at a pet store and
bought a fish tank for Tombo.

"What are we going to feed him?" asked Alex.

"We'll give him fish food," said Mom.

When they got home they made the fish tank ready for Tombo. When Alex put fish food into the tank, Tombo took one bite and said, "I hate this terrible, dried fish food. I demand my regular food! I'm *not* eating this!"

But that was all the food he got. Finally, Tombo became so hungry that he had to eat the dried fish food.

Every day Tombo swam around his tank, and
in the evenings he got more fish food. He hated
the food so much that he ate as little as possible.

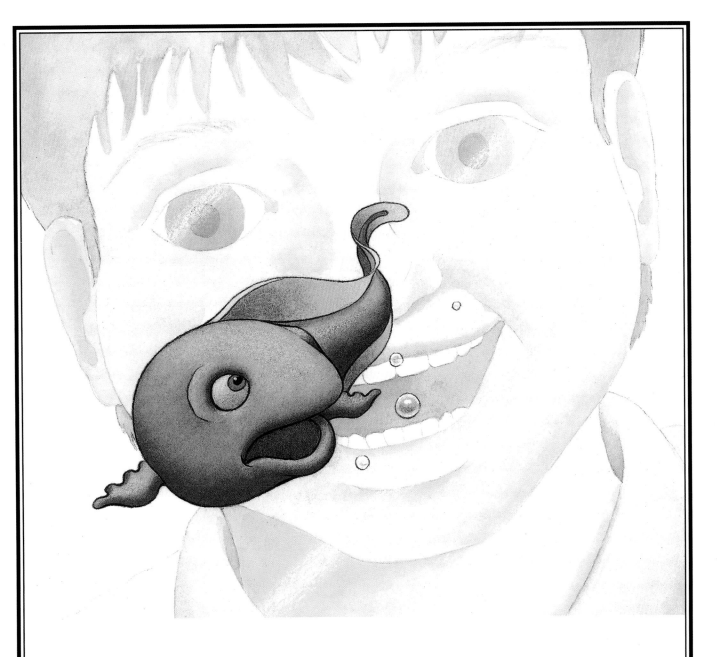

When Tombo took naps, Alex would often tap on the glass and say, "Let's see you swim, little tadpole."

Tombo would get so scared that he would dash across the tank. When he bumped his nose on the other side of the tank, he would yell, "Ouch!"

Alex thought it was so funny to see Tombo dash across the tank that he would laugh and laugh. But Tombo did not think it was the least bit funny. It made him mad.

One day as Alex was feeding Tombo, Alex called, "Mom, come quickly! Something strange is happening to my little tadpole!"

"What is it?" asked Mom.

"Something funny is growing out of my little tadpole."

"He's growing legs," said Mom.

"Growing legs?" asked a puzzled Alex. "How come I've never seen legs grow on people?"

"People are born with legs," explained Mom, "but tadpoles grow legs."

"I don't understand," said Alex.

"Let me tell you about tadpoles," said Mom. "A female frog lays eggs as the male frog fertilizes them. When the eggs hatch, tadpoles are born.

"These tadpoles breathe with gills under water, just like fish. They grow by eating algae, vegetation, and decaying animal matter.

"As tadpoles continue to grow, legs begin to form. First the back legs appear, then lungs develop, and then the front legs grow. The inside

of the tadpole also changes so it can eat flies,
mosquitoes, spiders, small fish, and earth-
worms. But when a tadpole loses its gills, it
must breathe air. It can no longer live under
water. That's when it becomes a frog."

"Wow!" said Alex shaking his head. "That's
amazing."

"It surely is," said Mom. "We live in a
wonderful and amazing world."

Alex watched as Tombo slowly began to change into a frog.

"When your tadpole turns into a little frog," said Mom, "we'll return him to his pond."

"I'm not turning into a little frog," fumed Tombo. "*I'm* going to be the biggest, the fastest, and the strongest frog! *I'm* King of the Pond!"

Finally, Tombo turned into a frog.

"Okay," said Mom, "your tadpole is now a little frog. Put him into a jar, and then we'll go to his pond to put him back."

Again Tombo was furious at being called "a *little* frog." But he was glad that he was going back to his own pond.

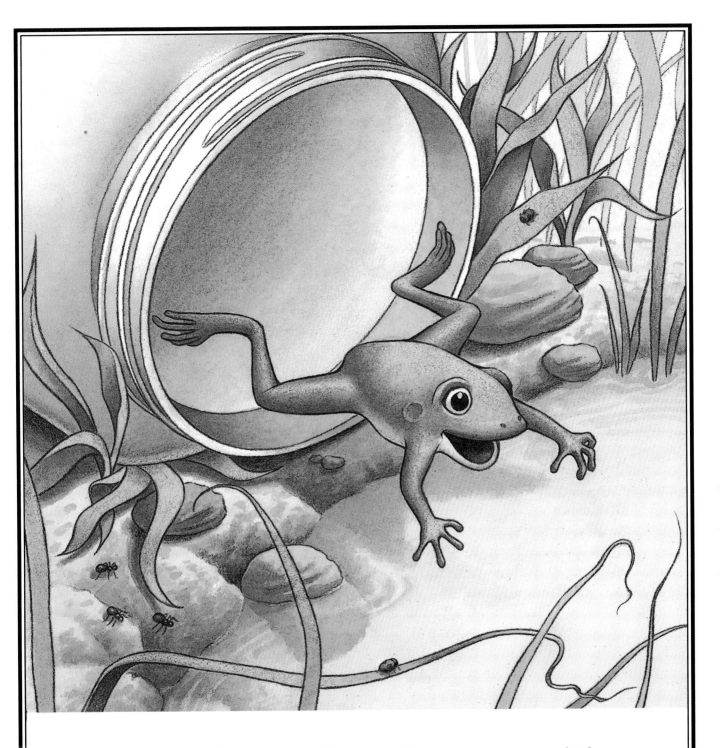

When Alex got to the pond, he unscrewed the lid and set the jar on the edge of the pond.

"Yippeeeee!" yelled Tombo as he jumped out of the jar and splashed into the pond. "I'll show them that *I'm* the biggest, the fastest, and the strongest frog! *I'm* King of the Pond!"

But Tombo did not realize that because he ate little, he grew little.

As Tombo swam away, some big frogs sped by him. They were having a race. Tombo tried to catch up with them, but he could not.

Tombo finally found them sitting on some lily pads. He jumped up on one too.

"Who are you?" asked one of the big frogs.

"I'm Tombo," he boasted. "*I'm* the biggest, the fastest, and the strongest frog! *I'm* King of the Pond!"

All the frogs laughed at him.

Tombo frowned and demanded from the frog next to him, "And who are you?"

"I'm Tilly."

"Tilly!" said Tombo in amazement. He could not believe what he saw. Then Tombo slowly turned around and asked the biggest frog of all, "An. . . An. . . And who are you?"

With a booming voice he said, "I'm Freddy. Don't you recognize me?"

"No," whispered Tombo.

Then Tombo realized that he was now the smallest, the slowest, and the weakest frog in the pond. He felt ashamed for the way he had treated his friends. Tombo lowered his head and said, "I'm sorry for the things I did to you."

"We forgive you," said all the frogs.

Tombo whispered, "Thank you," and then dove into the water to swim away.

"Come back!" yelled Tilly. "We want you to play with us."

Tombo swam back and played with them. He

had a great time. When they were finished playing, Tombo said to Tilly, "Now I know that having friends and treating them right is much more fun than being King of the Pond."

From then on the frogs had lots of fun playing together—and Tombo had the most fun of all.